For all our friends!

— *Ingrid & Dieter*

Copyright © 2015 by Lemniscaat, Rotterdam, The Netherlands

First published in The Netherlands under the title Opvrolijkvogeltje

Text copyright © 2015 by Edward van de Vendel

Illustration copyright © 2015 by Ingrid & Dieter Schubert

English translation copyright © 2015 by Lemniscaat USA LLC · New York

All rights reserved.

First published in the United States and Canada in 2015 by Lemniscaat USA LLC · New York

Distributed in the United States by Lemniscaat USA LLC · New York

Library of Congress Cataloging-in-Publication Data is available.

ISBN 13: 978-1-935954-45-3 (Hardcover)

Printing and binding: Worzalla, Stevens Point, WI USA

First U.S. edition

EDWARD VAN DE VENDEL

INGRID & DIETER SCHUBERT

The Cheer-up Bird

LEMNISCAAT ∞ USA

Look, it's Cheer-up Bird!
　Who?
Cheer-up Bird!
　What kind of bird is that?
It's an important bird.
　Why?

Morning had come again.
It was going to be a very busy day.

Three grumpy wombats sat in the playground.
One didn't want to play.
One couldn't play.
One wasn't allowed to play.

But then came **Cheer-up Bird!**

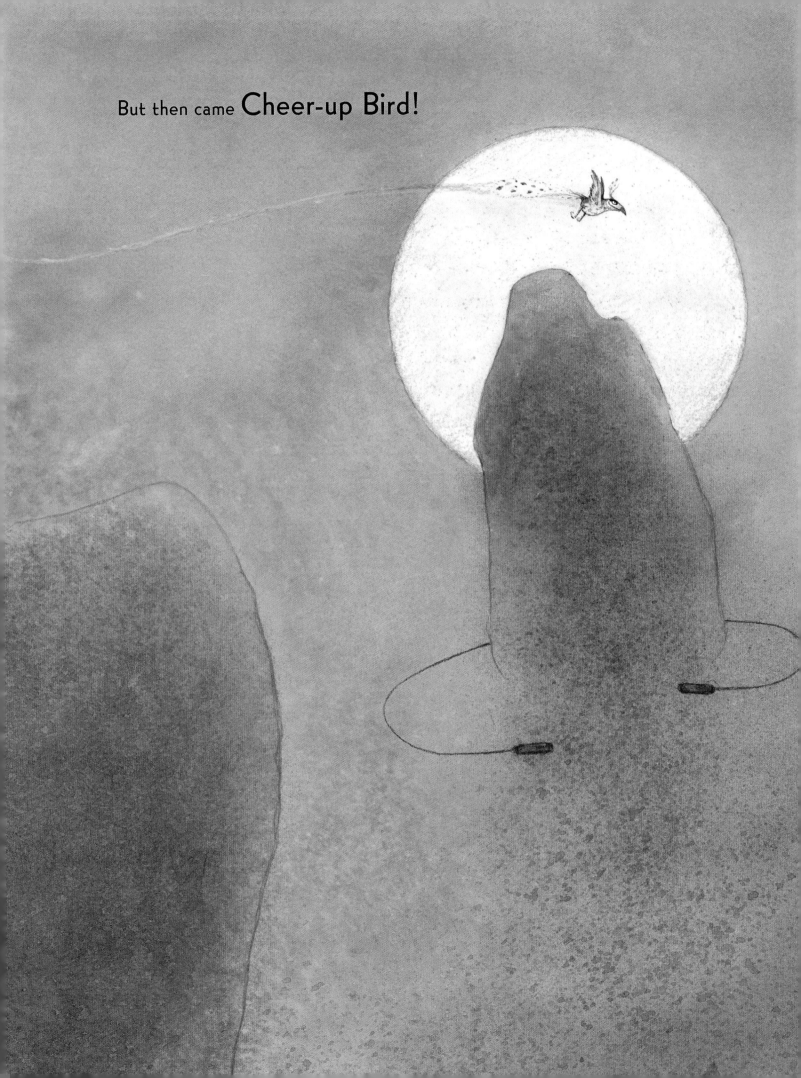

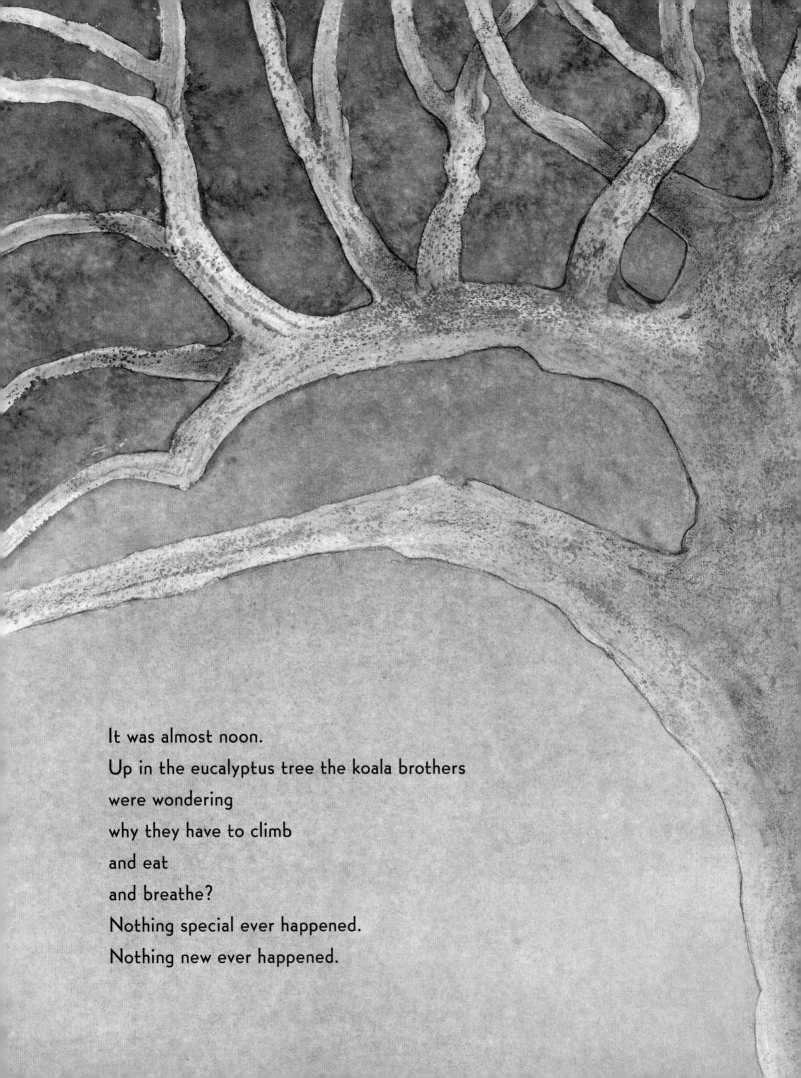

It was almost noon.
Up in the eucalyptus tree the koala brothers
were wondering
why they have to climb
and eat
and breathe?
Nothing special ever happened.
Nothing new ever happened.

But then came Cheer-up Bird!

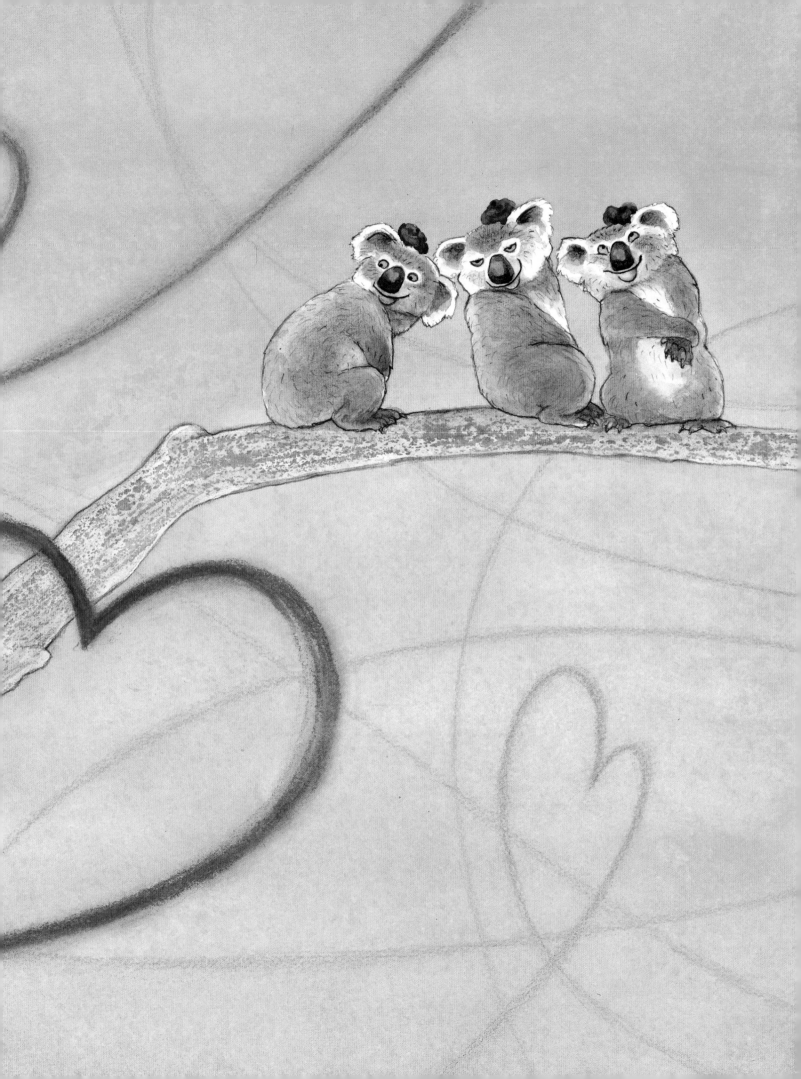

At the beginning of the afternoon, she had to visit kangaroo
who had been boss for a such a long time
that he became serious and gloomy.

But then came Cheer-up Bird!

It was the end of the afternoon,
and Cheer-up Bird's work wasn't over yet.

There were Emu Grandpa and Emu Grandma.
Even their rocking chairs were too tired to move!

But then came Cheer-up Bird!

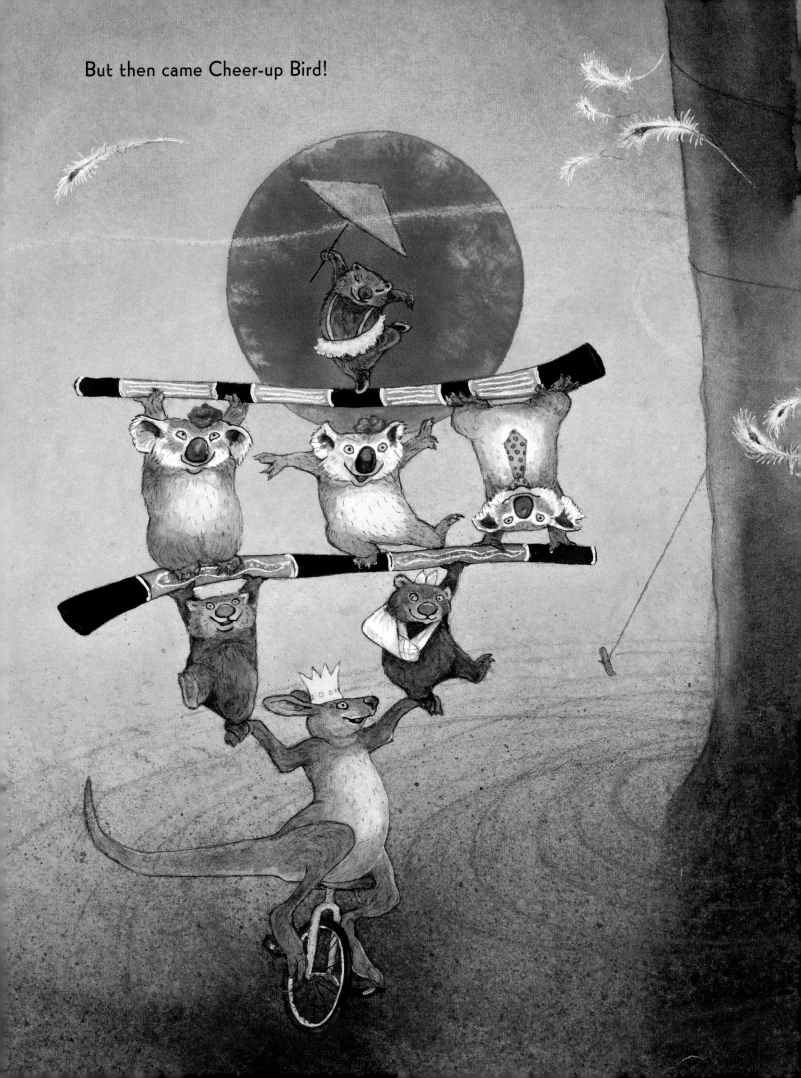

It was evening and everyone was happy.

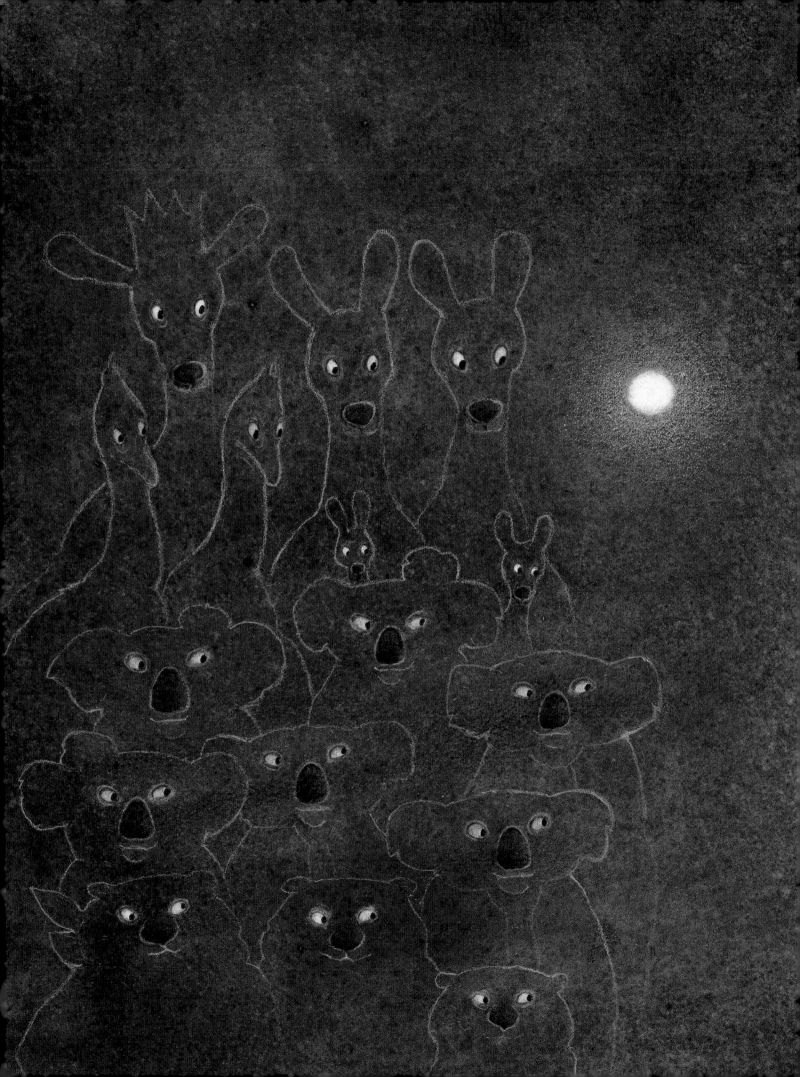

Everyone, except Cheer-up Bird.
No, she wasn't.
    Why not?
Cheer-up Bird had been working all day. She was so tired.
She really wanted to be at home, and she was not home yet.
    That is so sad.
    She looks gloomy herself now.
    Tomorrow she must get back to work.
    Will she be able to?
Yes, she will...
    How?

Finally Cheer-up Bird reached her nest.
With her last strength, she tumbled in.

And then they are there.

Her cheery Cheer-up Bird Birdies!

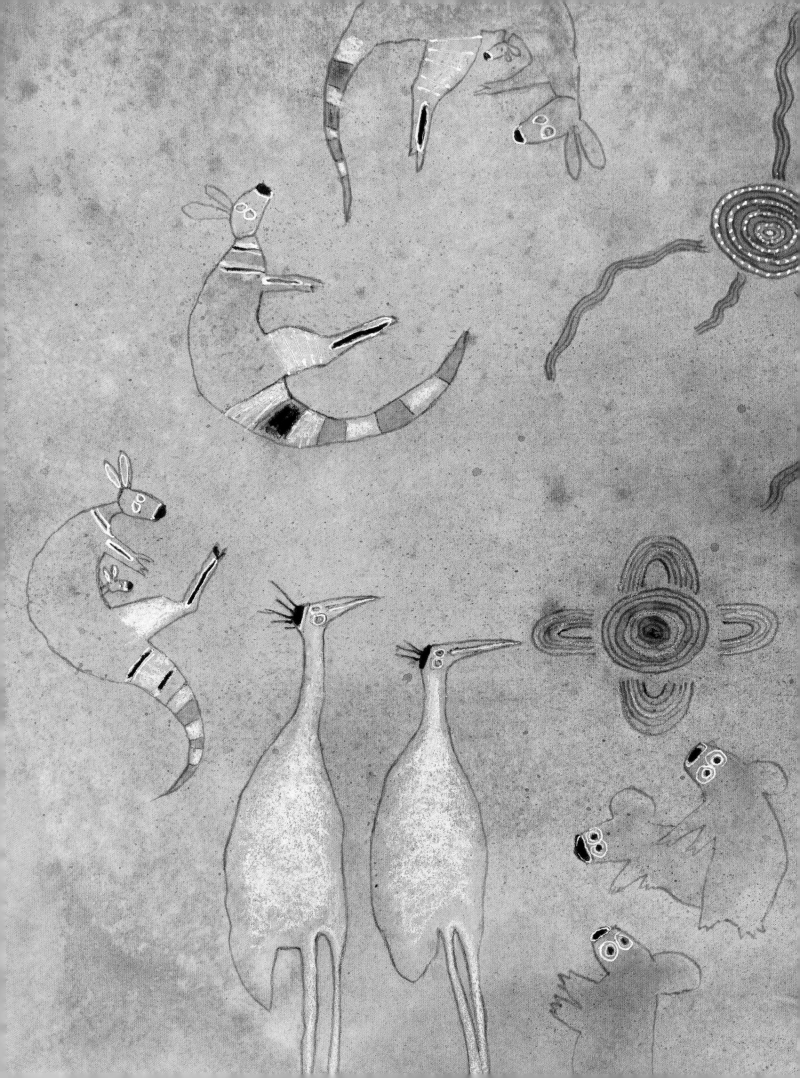